Do you have a problem?

Wise old Hildegarde the owl

will gladly advise you.

Write at once

to your friend

in need,

everyone's friend

indeed,

Dear Hildegarde.

by BERNARD WABER

Dear Hildegarde:

Round Meadow School Library
Calabasas, California

Houghton
Mifflin
Company
Boston
1980

for
PAULIS
and
ROD

L. of C. Cat. Card No. 80-13262
ISBN 0-395-29745-1

Copyright © 1980 by Bernard Waber
Printed in the United States of America.
P   10   9   8   7   6   5   4   3   2   1

And now, dear readers,

my first letter.

A dog writes . . .

Dear Hildegarde:

Why are dogs given human names?

Take my name for example —

please . . .

BETTER
TO BE WISE
THAN
OTHERWISE

It's Bernard.

Now, isn't that a ridiculous name—

I mean, for a dog?

And I don't even look

like a Bernard.

Yet, day after day,

all I ever hear is:

"Sit, Bernard! Sit!

Beg, Bernard! Beg!

Catch, Bernard! Catch!

Walk, Bernard! Walk!

Roll, Bernard! Roll!

Good, Bernard! Good!"

Yecch! What's so good about it!

Hildegarde, why couldn't I have been given

a decent dog name—

something interesting like:

Rover, Spot, Champ, or Prince?

Come to think of it,

I do look most like a Prince.

Signed,

Any name but Bernard

Hildegarde replies . . .

Dear Any:

You are not alone.

My mail grows heartbreakingly heavy

with this particular problem.

Perhaps, if you do not answer to the

name Bernard, others will take the hint

and know, where you are concerned,

they are simply barking

up the wrong tree.

A giraffe writes . . .

Dear Hildegarde:

No doubt you have already guessed —

my problem is

I am extraordinarily tall.

And because I am so tall,
I will sometimes pass smaller
friends by without really
seeing them.

Hildegarde, is it my fault I cannot
always see what goes on beneath
my very own nose?

Lately, these so-called "friends"

accuse me of behaving in an uppity manner,

of always having my head in the clouds.

How can I make them understand?

Would it help if I stooped to their level?

Signed,

Stuck—up

Hildegarde replies . . .

Dear Stuck:

Don't stoop.

Just continue being your own

sweet uplifting self.

Your "true" friends

will understand.

A pig writes . . .

Dear Hildegarde:

Does anyone care to know how pigs feel when

they hear insulting remarks like:

pig-headed,

piggish,

fat-as-a-pig,

dirty pig?

Don't you agree, these remarks place

pigs in a very poor light?

And what must our young piglets
think of themselves, having always
to hear this kind of swill?

I, for one, am fed up with it—

especially about pigs being dirty.

Let's set the record straight.

Pigs are not dirty.

Yes, it is true —

true, true, true —

we enjoy a certain amount

of frisking in the mud.

What of it?

And doesn't everyone?

Rolling about in mud happens to be
clean, gorgeous, exhilarating fun—
and mighty healthy for the soul.
I recommend it highly.
And as for those so-called "messy"
eating habits . . .
well, dear Hildegarde . . .

try having *your* dinner
served from a trough.
Signed,
Disgruntled

Hildegarde replies . . .

Dear Disgruntled:

Each week, hundreds of letters cross

my desk with the same sad complaint—

not only from pigs like yourself,

but from other animal friends.

Isn't it time this ugly name-calling

was stopped?

Isn't it time we heard the last of

stupid cow,

sly fox,

stubborn mule,

old goat,

daffy loon,

silly jackass,

dirty rat?

But why go on?

A bird writes . . .

Dear Hildegarde:

My mate (I'll call him Gus) and I have

been building a nest.

But actually, I have been doing

all of the work.

Gus hasn't done a thing. Not one

solitary thing.

He is no help whatsoever.

All Gus does is perch himself

on a branch and whistle his song.

Believe me, Hildegarde, when I tell you

building a nest is no picnic.

It's hard, hard work.

Day after day, I must fly about

gathering twigs, roots, and bark

to strengthen the nest . . .

horsehair to tighten it . . .

pellets of mud

to plaster

its walls . . .

and chicken feathers to give it

a soft, warm bedding.

And any day now,
I'll be having all those
eggs to lay.

One day, when I had my fill of it,

I confronted Gus.

I said,

"Gus, you haven't done one stitch

of work around the nest.

All you do is whistle that

everlasting song of yours."

"I beg your pardon," said Gus.

"For your information,

whistling is work—important work.

It's my *job* to whistle.

When I whistle, I am warning other birds

to stay away. I am protecting the nest.

And doing it splendidly, if I

must say so myself."

Hildegarde, this really got my feathers up.

"Who said whistling is work!" I exclaimed.

"Any fool can whistle!

Whistling is not work!

Work is work!"

"Sorry," said Gus, "I didn't make

the rules."

Hildegarde, do you think it's fair?

Gus knows I am writing to you.

Signed,

Who made the rules?

Hildegarde replies . . .

Dear Who:

Rules can be changed —

and so must Gus's tune.

Ask Gus if he has ever heard of

whistling while you work.

A spider writes . . .

Dear Hildegarde:

All of my friends, everyone my age,

spin these really beautiful,

dreamy webs.

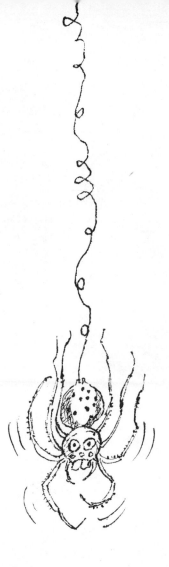

But somehow, I can't seem to
get the hang of it.

Each time I try to spin a web,
I end up a sorry tangled mess.

Most of these friends have already
trapped their first fly.

Yesterday, I overheard someone remark,

"What self-respecting fly would want

to crawl into that?" —

meaning, of course, my web.

Hildegarde, what's wrong with me?

Signed,

All in knots

Hildegarde replies . . .

Dear All In:

Yours is a rather sticky problem.

But think of it this way:

Your web is like no other web

in the whole wide world.

Be proud of it.

It's you.

Weave on!

A beaver writes . . .

Dear Hildegarde:

Please print this letter so others

will read it and, perhaps,

understand my problem.

I am in the building business—dams.

And I work nights.

Night after night

I am out there, chewing

down trees, stripping branches,

carrying load upon load

of wood to the lake.

By the time dawn rolls around,

I am exhausted,

and ready for sleep.

But that's my problem.

Each time I begin to fall asleep,

I am jolted awake by noisy,

screeching, chattering,

inconsiderate neighbors.

Hildegarde, I can't go on.

This is my busy season.

I must have sleep.

Signed,

It's a jungle out there

Hildegarde replies . . .

Dear It's:

I'm rather a night person myself
and can fully appreciate your problem.
But it's too late to change the
sleeping habits of the world.
Perhaps you should consider moving
to a quieter neighborhood.

A moth writes . . .

Dear Hildegarde:

I write to you in tears and shame.
Hildegarde, I know it makes no sense
whatsoever, but every time I see a
lighted bulb, something comes over me,
some madness that makes me want to
throw myself at it, kick it, bump it,
whack it, rage at it.

Don't ask me why.
I've asked myself that same miserable
question over and over again.

A moth writes . . .

Dear Hildegarde:

I write to you in tears and shame.

Hildegarde, I know it makes no sense

whatsoever, but every time I see a

lighted bulb, something comes over me,

some madness that makes me want to

throw myself at it, kick it, bump it,

whack it, rage at it.

Don't ask me why.

I've asked myself that same miserable

question over and over again.

But that's my problem.

Each time I begin to fall asleep,

I am jolted awake by noisy,

screeching, chattering,

inconsiderate neighbors.

Hildegarde, I can't go on.

This is my busy season.

I must have sleep.

Signed,

It's a jungle out there

Hildegarde repli

Dear It's:

I'm rather a nigh

and can fully ap

But it's too late

sleeping habits

Perhaps you sh

to a quieter nei

Night after night,

it's the same tragic story.

You'll find me at some silly light bulb —

KICKING! BUMPING! WHACKING! WHAMMING!

WHOMPING! ZOOMING! CRASHING!

And when merciful daylight arrives,

I fly away on singed wings

and with a heavy heart,

asking myself,

"Why? Why? Why?"

Oh, Hildegarde,

is there help for me?

Signed,

Why do I do these crazy things?

P.S.

Knowing that others share this

problem is not helpful.

Hildegarde replies . . .

Dear Why:

I don't know why. I am still in the
dark about this light bulb disturbance.
But I can see where your life
needs brightening.
I would advise that you switch to
new outlets.
Seek out exciting friendships.
Join in serving the needy.
Spend time wisely on hobbies
or projects.
Only by learning to keep busy,
will you begin to see the "true" light.

And so, dear readers,

we come to the end of another

busy, busy day.

Tomorrow, I will return

with more lovely, lovely problems.

Meanwhile, do try to keep in mind:

Behind every dark cloud,

there is a golden ray of hope and cheer.

And if you, too, have a problem,

don't hesitate,

send a letter—or even a card,

to old, and astonishingly wise,

Dear Hildegarde.